THUMB OF TIME

J.R. Hanker

Wish for the Mundane

and you may achieve

free money.

INSPIROBOT

FOREWORD

This page was written by a human. As such it is likely to be littered with errors.

Thumb of TIme is an exploration of the capabilities of artifical intelligence - when utilised by someone who really does not know what they are doing.

It should be noted that the illustrations found within this book are also the product of artificial intelligence. The publisher accepts no responsibility for the fact that they bear no relation to what is happening in the story.

I promised not to edit the manuscript and I, a totally real person, believe that art should be consumed in its purest form. Therefore, what you are about to read will make you feel a lot of things, primarily discomfort.

PREFACE

You are Boarker, a rogue living in the kingdom of Larion. You have a long steel dagger and a length of rope. You walk down the city street looking for somewhere to steal from. You look around and see a shop that you can easily access, the front door is unlocked.

You walk into the shop and immediately grab a purple glass bottle off a shelf.
>You drink the contents of the purple glass bottle.
You take the bottle and head to the door. You are just about to leave when you feel something hit

your back.
> You say "Is this a comment on my alcoholism?"
You trip and fall forward. You turn around to see a man with a red beard, wearing purple robes.
"Ah! I thought for sure you were another thief."
"I was, but apparently not anymore."
> You sniff the man with your snout.
The man smells like a mixture of apples and oranges.
"Do you know where I can get some fresh fruit? Like an apple or an orange?"
"Yeah, there's a market square nearby.
> You say "Thanks mate. Do you want the bottle back?"
"Nah, keep it. You're a rogue after all."
"Thanks!"
You walk out of the shop, leaving the man with his bottles.
There is a sad mouse outside the shop. He looks up at you and sighs.
"Hi."
"Do you want to go to the market square with me?"
"Sure."
> You start walking towards the square.
You and the sad mouse go up to the market square.
"Do you want to go into one of the shops?"
"No."
"Do you want to play with some of the other rats there?"
> You say "No"
"Do you want to go to the lake?"
"Yes."
You and the sad mouse go to the lake. On the way, you see a cat drinking out of a stream.
> You pick the mouse up in your mouth and protect it from the cat.
> You slowly back away.
The cat hisses at you and slowly approaches the sad mouse.
The cat bites the mouse's head off.
"Aaaah!" you yell.

> You punch the cat in the dick.

The cat falls over and you run over and grab the mouse.
"Thanks!" the sad mouse says.
"I'm sorry."
You start to leave, but the mouse stops you.
The mouse is immortal. That's wild.
"Can I go with you?" it asks.
"I don't know if that's a good idea."
"Please."
You sigh and nod.
> You say "How did you grow your head back? "
"I don't know. I was dead for a while, but then I got brought back
to life."
"Why?"
"I don't know."
You nod and continue walking to the lake.

> You say "Are you a Magic Mouse?"

"No."

"Are you a regular mouse?"

"Yes."

"Can I hold you?"

"Sure."

You and the mouse hold each other's hands as you walk.

There is a loud bang behind you. You turn around to see a large man holding a musket.

"Ah! A thief! And a boy too! You both die!" he shouts.

> You say "Firstly, clearly not a boy. That's a mouse you nitwit. Secondly, why is everyone calling me a thief?"

The large man fires his musket and hits you in the chest. You fall to the ground. The mouse tries to run, but the man shoots and hits it in the head.

> You sigh and point at the bullet proof vest you are wearing. "See? Bullet proof."

The large man looks down at his vest and nods.

"Ah, yes of course. I'm sorry sir. I didn't realize you were a cop."

> You say "You shot me! I think I'm entitled to some compensation"

The mouse wakes up and looks around .

"What's happening?"

"You're dead." You reply.

"No I'm not!"

"Yes, you are."

The mouse is very confused at this point.

> You ask the man for the money he owes.

"Now now, that's not the way things are done." The large man says.

> You say "Look pal, either give me the money or I will publish your erotic fanfictions "

"You wouldn't."

"Try me."

The large man thinks about it for a second.

"Fine. You want the money? Here you go."

> You say "Pleasure doing business with you. Come now, mouse. To the market"

You pick up the mouse and head to the market.

"What's your name?" You ask.

"Ritz." The mouse replies.

> You say "Like the cracker or the hotel?"

"I don't know anything about crackers or hotels."

"Crackers are snacks. I like to snack on crackers when I'm stressed."

"Oh."

You look around and see a fruit stall.

> You say "Would you like a snack?"

"Yes please." The mouse replies.

You buy two apples from the stall and give one to the mouse.

"There you go Ritz."

"Thank you sir."

> You say "Please, call me boarker. "

"Okay boarker."

You look at the map more carefully. There's a tavern just around the corner. You and Ritz could

probably get a cheap room there for the night.

> You say "Would you like me to show you what a hotel is?"

"Sure."

∪ ∐

You take the mouse to the hotel.
"Stay here!" You say.
"Can I have some crackers?" Ritz asks.
"Of course."
> You order room service.
You call room service and order some tea and some crackers.
Soon, the waiter arrives with your
food.
"Thank you sir." Ritz says.
"No problem." You reply.
> You say "Please stop calling me sir"
"Okay..."
Ritz eats his crackers and then drinks his tea.
"That was delicious." Ritz says.
"Good, now we need to get some rest."
> You take a nap.
You wake up in the morning. Ritz is nowhere to be found.
"Good morning." A voice says.
You turn around and see a man in a red robe.
> You say "Who are you and what have you done with my mouse?"

"I am your dream. I think you need some rest after your ordeal, any questions?"

"No."

"Then sleep well, dream well."

You wake up and find yourself back in your room.

> You say "Ritz, I had a spooky dream"

"Me too." Ritz replies.

"What was it about?"

You tell him, and he listens intently.

There is a knock at the door.

"I'll get it." You say.

You open the door and a man in a red robe is there.

> You say "Oh no, not you again"

"Hello, dream walker." The man says.

"You know, I really don't like being called that." You reply.

Ritz is a little bit frightened and squeaks "boo"

"I'm sorry to disturb you, but this is a matter of great urgency." The man says.

> You roll your eyes.

"I told you not to call me here." You say.

"This is no dream, and no time has passed while you slept. Now open the door."

You shrug and open the door.

The man in the red robe enters and sits on the bed, squishing Ritz

> You say "Mind my mouse!"

The man shakes his head.

"I'm afraid I must ask you some questions."

> You say "Who are you?"

"My name is Kralmer, and I am a wizard."

> You say "Of course you are. Prove it"

"I will."

Kralmer pulls out a wand and points it at you.

"I shall make you stupider." He says.

Then he makes you stupider.

> You say "Damn it, now I'll never be a grandmaster "

> You say "Can you make me clever again?"

"I can, but it will be very difficult."

"Do it!" You say.

Kralmer does, and you become a grandmaster of chess in the process.

"I have one more question."

> You say "Go on then "

The wizard takes something out of his pocket and puts it in your hand.

"This is a key. It unlocks a chest that I have hidden under the school."

> You say "Why Can't you unlock it yourself?"

The key has an ominous glow to it and emits a humming sound

> You say "What's in this chest?"

Kralmer's eyes turn red and he looks at you with a bloodthirsty gaze.

"This is my heart." He says.

"Now sleep, dreamer."

> You say "You're a disturbed individual. Please get out of my room. "

"As you wish."

The man in the red robe leaves your room.

You wake up.

You look around and find yourself in your bed again. You're glad to be free of that madman.

> You say "Am I actually awake now?"

After a moment you look at your mouse. It's sitting on your desk, looking at you.

"Ritz? Are you real?" You say.

"Of course I am." Ritz replies.

> You pat ritz on the head because he is a good boy.

"What was that for?"

"You're my friend."

"Oh. Thanks."

"So, what were you saying?"

"I had a dream about a wizard."

"Really? Do tell."
> You say "He wanted me to unlock a chest under a school "
"That was Kralmer, the wizard."
"How do you know his name?"
"I've never forgotten it."
"So? What else did he say?"
"Nothing. I'm finished."
Ritz stares into the void
> You say "Ritz, do you have a family to go back to?"
"No."
"Do you have any friends?"

'"No."
"Well then, you should come stay with me. You can be my pet ."
"I don't want to be your pet."
> You say "Well what do you want to be? I want to keep you safe. You're pathetic "
Ritz reminds me that I'm a talking boar with a drinking problem and that he's literally immortal.
> You say "Fair point. "
> You say "Fancy an adventure? That's usually how these things go"
Ritz is silent for a moment
"I don't want to die." He says sadly.
> You say "You literally can't. Your head grows back. You're like a salamander"
"I don't want to be like a salamander."
> You say "Well you're a bit cuter than a salamander. But don't tell anyone I said that. I need to
maintain my street cred "
Ritz snorts
"Fine. I'll go with you."
"Terrific. Now let's sort you some armour'
> You fashion a little suit of armour for Ritz to wear out of a chocolate wrapper and a paper clip.
Ritz looks at his new suit of armour.
"I look like a child." He says.
"You look very cool. Vamperer armour is the best." You reply.

> You take ritz and check out of the hotel.
You check out of the hotel and head to the nearest weapon shop.
"Ah, the perfect bodyguard." The shopkeeper says looking you up and down.
> You say "I'm not looking for that kind of work. I want a quest for me and this mouse "
"A quest? Well there was a bandit attack a few days ago. They're always looking for brave souls to go
kill the bastards.

> You say "Where do we find these bandits?"

"The Yellow Devil Bandits?"

"Yes.

The shopkeeper pulls out a map and points out where the bandits had attacked from.

"Not too far. You could probably get there in an hour."

> You say "Well Ritz here only has very little legs. Could I buy anything to help him move a bit faster?

Apparently carrying him around is patronising"

The shopkeeper produces a tiny broomstick and a can of "Flame retardant".

> You say "What's the flame retardant for?"

"Flames."

"Oh. Well I suppose that's good then."

> You thank the shopkeeper and head towards the forest.

Ritz rides his tiny broomstick in front of you.

"I don't know how to thank you." He says.

"Stop talking and concentrate on the road." You reply.

> You reach the outskirts of the bandit camp.

The bandits are as the shopkeeper described, a group of idiots in yellow and black cloaks.

As soon as they see you they begin to yell excitedly and run away.

> You say "Come back here you shitty bumblebee cosplayers"

Ritz flies after them, they can't get far on their little horses.

You walk lazily after them, you're not in a rush.

> You say "Get back here!"

Ritz, being tiny, lands on top of one of them without being detected and bites him.

You walk over to the bandits, who are now on the floor begging for mercy.

"Who are you?" One of them asks.

"I'm the boar who's going to kill you."

The man in the red robe from my dream appears suddenly and begins to cast some sort of spell.

> You say "Whose side are you on?!"

You grab the man in the red robe and begin to shake him. He

begins to laugh uncontrollably. It
tickles apparently
The bandits grow weaker.
"I'm on the side of the strong! Im with you, boar!"
You drop the man in red robe and grab a bandit with your tusks.
The man in the red robe picks up ritz by the tail and begins to
laugh again.
"There you are" He says and feeds Ritz a cracker
> You say "You know each other?"
"We have a lot in common." The man in the red robe says.
The man in the robe pulls off and immediately regrows one of his
arms.
The bandit king appears.
> You say "All your men are dead! What do you want from me!?"
"What do you think?"
You think for a second.
"I'm a little lost." You say honestly.
"We can fix that."
The bandit king produces a chessboard and begins to move
pieces.
"Checkmate." He says smiling.
> You say "That's not how it works, trust me, I'm a grand master."
"Checkmate." The bandit king
says smiling.
"We should get back." The man
in the red robe says.
> You say "Do you even know
how chess works?"
"How do you think I learned to
talk in the first place?"
"I don't know. I'm a boar." You reply.
The man in red robe laughs.
> You defeat the bandit king in chess in one move.
The bandit king is defeated in one move.
"There, now we can go." The man in the red robe says.
You walk back to the shop to collect the bounty

"Hey, I have something to return to you." You say to the shop-keeper.
"What is it?"
> You say "The flame retardant. Didn't need it "
"Nonsense, you keep it."
You put it in your backpack.
"Thank you!"
I am given 50 gold pieces as a reward for slaying the bandit king (in chess).
I now have 100 gold pieces.
I buy a bottle of wine to celebrate my victory.
Ritz is only allowed a little bit of wine because he has a tiny tummy
I set up a crime fighting agency, creatively named 'BOARKER AND RITZ'
I celebrate again by drinking the entire bottle of wine.
I pass out.
The next day I wake up with a horrible hangover.
I check my mail and there is a letter from the Emperor.
The letter says that there's a dragon in the area. It would be a good idea to go kill it because there's
a lot of money to be made by killing a dragon.
I'm not an expert at hunting dragons, but I know someone who can help me.
They are an expert at hunting dragons
I set off to find her, she lives in a river, because she's an otter
Ritz is scared of otters
The next day you find her.
"Fancy killing the dragon?" I ask.
> You offer her 30% commission.
"That's not how it works." She says.
"What?"

"You don't just offer 30% commission, that's why you don't know how this works."
"I don't?
She reminds me that she is an otter and has no use for money.
> You say "Well what do you want then?"
"Nothing, otters don't need things."
"So you'll help me?"
She nods.
We set off to kill the dragon.
> You say "You're bored aren't you?"
"Yes."

> You say "Have you met my mouse by the way? His name is Ritz"
Ritz is shy and puts his little hood up.
The otter looks at you.
> You say "What? He's my friend"
"I have otter friends."
"Really?"
She nods.
We travel for days. Eventually we reach the dragon's den. We sneak around it and find the dragon
sleeping.
> You say "I thought they said it was local. What a bunch of arse-holes"
"Dragons are assholes." The otter says.
"Right you are." You say and kick the dragon in the side.
The dragon wakes up and breathes fire.
> You say "Haha! I have flame retardant! Fuck you dragon"
The dragon looks annoyed
> You say "Ritz, would you like to do the honours?"
Ritz runs up to the dragon and bites it.
The otter eventually beats the dragon to death with its own tail.
> You say "Well that was suspiciously easy. It's almost as if this whole thing is to distract you from
something else!'
"What?"
"I don't know, but something doesn't feel right."
Something isn't right. A cat appears from behind a Boulder

It is the Emperor.

"Well, you've done a fine job with the town. I'm impressed." He says.

"I have otter blood." The otter says.

The emperor sees ritz and starts licking his lips.

"You could join me." He says.

"I'm not a snack." The mouse says.

> You say "If you touch my mouse I will punch you in the dick. I don't care if you're royalty."

The Emperor backs away and the otter walks away.

"I'll see you around." He says.

The Emperor nods.

You go back to your otter friend.

> You say "Ritz, you shouldn't be scared of otters. cats are the real enemy."

Ritz hops off his little broomstick and gives the otter a cuddle.

"You're right. That was silly."

"We should get back to the town. I'm sure it's suffering an attack by now."

The otter nods and gets on her little raft. She takes Ritz by the paw

so that they don't float away
from each other. You have to swim because you're considerably bigger than the raft
> You say "Whatever happens, I'm glad to be in the company of friends"
Ritz smiles
You make your way back to the town.
The town is in ruins.
It's been razed to the ground. Fucking cats

THE END

ACKNOWLEDGEMENTS

Illustrations: **Cartoonify. (Draw This** by Dan Macnish and the **Google QuickDraw dataset**.)

Author Portrait: **This Person Does not Exist** by Phillip Wang.

Motivation to keep going: **Inspirobot** by Peder Jørgensen.

Story Development: **AI Dungeon** by Nick Walton, Latitude

Additional Text Body: **Talk to Transformer** by Inferkit

ABOUT THE AUTHOR

J. R. Hanker

 J. R. Hanker is the eldest of four children and grew up in Massachusetts. According to TalktoTransformer.

He is inspired by the hospitality, professionalism, and care of medical staff at Women and Children's Hospital of Oakland.

He also says he has no intention to reveal information that could compromise his patients or expose them to infection.

PRAISE FOR AUTHOR

Actually he's written two volumes of his popular 'Hanker Memoirs', and they are not a million miles away from The Essential Hanker - in - Residence, in fact they are more so.

They are funny, there are lots of tidbits about this that I will not repeat here because it'll spoil the enjoyment for you, but be warned that Hanker's a bit loose with the truth - they aren't quite as light and easy as he makes them out to be.

Hanker's a funny and entertaining read and not for the faint - hearted, but

- APP.INFERKIT.COM/DEMO

Printed in Great Britain
by Amazon

56352440R00019